3 Great Offers For Mr Men Fans

1 Token EGMONT WORLD

1 FREE Door Hangers and Posters

In every Mr Men and Little Miss Book like this one you will find a special token. Collect 6 and we will send you either a brilliant Mr. Men or Little Miss poster and a Mr Men or Little Miss double sided, full colour, bedroom door hanger. Apply using the coupon overleaf, enclosing six tokens and a 50p coin for your choice of two items.

Egmont World tokens can be used towards any other Egmont World / World International token scheme promotions., in early learning and story / activity books.

Posters: Tick your preferred choice of either Mr Men ☐ or Little Miss ☐

Door Hangers: Choose from: Mr. Nosey & Mr Muddle ☐, Mr Greedy & Mr Lazy ☐, Mr Tickle & Mr Grumpy ☐, Mr Slow & Mr Busy ☐, Mr Messy & Mr Quiet ☐, Mr Perfect & Mr Forgetful ☐, Little Miss Fun & Little Miss Late ☐, Little Miss Helpful & Little Miss Tidy ☐, Little Miss Busy & Little Miss Brainy ☐, Little Miss Star & Little Miss Fun ☐. (Please tick)

2 Mr Men Library Boxes

Keep your growing collection of Mr Men and Little Miss books in these superb library boxes. With an integral carrying handle and stay-closed fastener, these full colour, plastic boxes are fantastic. They are just £5.49 each including postage. Order overleaf.

3 Join The Club

To join the fantastic Mr Men & Little Miss Club, check out the page overleaf NOW!

D1016080

MR MEN and LITTLE MISS™ & © 1998 Mrs. Roger Hargreaves

Join Our Club!

MR. MEN & Little Miss CLUB

When you become a member of the fantastic Mr Men and Little Miss Club you'll receive a personal letter from Mr Happy and Little Miss Giggles, a club badge with your name, and a superb Welcome Pack (pictured below right).

You'll also get birthday and Christmas cards from the Mr Men and Little Misses, 2 newsletters crammed with special offers, privileges and news, and a copy of the 12 page Mr Men catalogue which includes great party ideas.

If it were on sale in the shops, the Welcome Pack alone might cost around £13. But a year's membership is just £9.99 (plus 73p postage) with a 14 day money-back guarantee if you are not delighted!

HOW TO APPLY To apply for any of these three great offers, ask an adult to complete the coupon below and send it with appropriate payment and tokens (where required) to: Mr Men Offers, PO Box 7, Manchester M19 2HD. Credit card orders for Club membership ONLY by telephone, please call: 01403 242727.

To be completed by an adult

❑ **1.** Please send a poster and door hanger as selected overleaf. I enclose six tokens and a 50p coin for post (coin not required if you are also taking up 2. or 3. below).

❑ **2.** Please send __ Mr Men Library case(s) and __ Little Miss Library case(s) at £5.49 each.

❑ **3.** Please enrol the following in the Mr Men & Little Miss Club at £10.72 (inc postage)

Fan's Name:_____Fan's Address:_____

_____Post Code:_____Date of birth:__/__/__

Your Name:_____Your Address:_____

Post Code:_____Name of parent or guardian (if not you):_____

Total amount due: £_____ (£5.49 per Library Case, £10.72 per Club membership)

❑ I enclose a cheque or postal order payable to Egmont World Limited.

❑ Please charge my MasterCard / Visa account.

Card number: | | | | | | | | | | | | | | | | |

Expiry Date: ____/____   Signature: _____

Data Protection Act: If you do **not** wish to receive other family offers from us or companies we recommend, please tick this box ❑. Offer applies to UK only

little Miss Sunshine

by Roger Hargreaves

WORLD INTERNATIONAL

Welcome to Miseryland.

We say 'welcome', but there really isn't very much to welcome you about it.

It's the most miserable place in the world.

Miseryland worms look like this!

And when the birds wake up in the morning in Miseryland, they don't start singing.

They start crying!

Oh, it really is an awful place!

And the King of Miseryland is even worse.

He sits on his throne all day long with tears streaming down his face.

"Oh I'm so unhappy," he keeps sobbing, over and over and over again.

Dear, oh dear, oh dear!

Little Miss Sunshine had been on holiday.

She'd had a lovely time, and now she was driving home.

She was whistling happily to herself as she drove along when, out of the corner of her eye, she saw a signpost.

To Miseryland.

"Miseryland?" she thought to herself.

"I've never heard of that before!"

And she turned off down the road.

She came to a sign which read:

YOU ARE NOW ENTERING MISERYLAND

And underneath it said:

SMILING

LAUGHING

CHUCKLING

GIGGLING

FORBIDDEN

By Order of the King.

"Oh dear," thought little Miss Sunshine as she drove along.

She came to a castle with a huge door.

A soldier stopped her.

"What do you want?" he asked gloomily.

"I want to see the King," smiled little Miss Sunshine.

"You're under arrest," said the soldier.

"But why?" asked little Miss Sunshine.

"For a most serious crime," replied the soldier.

"Most serious indeed!"

The soldier marched little Miss Sunshine through the huge door.

And across a courtyard.

And through another huge door.

And up an enormous staircase.

And along a long corridor.

And through another huge door.

And into a gigantic room.

And at the end of the gigantic room sat the King.

Crying his eyes out!

"Your Majesty," said the soldier, bowing low, "I have arrested this person for a most serious crime!"

The King stopped crying.

"She smiled at me," said the soldier.

There was a shocked silence.

"She did WHAT?" cried the King.

"She smiled at me," repeated the soldier.

"But why is smiling not allowed?" laughed little Miss Sunshine.

"She LAUGHED at me," cried the King.

"Why not?" she chuckled.

"She CHUCKLED!" cried the King.

Little Miss Sunshine giggled.

"She GIGGLED!" went on the King.

And he burst into tears again.

"But why are these things not allowed?"
asked little Miss Sunshine.

"Because this is Miseryland," wept the King.

"And they've never been allowed," he sobbed.

"Oh, I was so unhappy before you arrived,"
he wailed, "but now I'm twice as unhappy!"

Little Miss Sunshine looked at him.

"But wouldn't you like to be happy?"
she asked.

"Of course I would," cried the King.

"But how can I be? This is MISERYLAND!"

Little Miss Sunshine thought.

"Come on," she said.

"You can't talk to me like that," sobbed the King.

"Don't be silly," she replied, and led him across the gigantic room, and through the huge door, and along the long corridor, and down the enormous staircase, and through the huge door, and across the courtyard, and through the huge door, to her car.

"Get in," she said.

Little Miss Sunshine drove the crying King back to the large notice.

"Dry your eyes," she said, and handed him a large handkerchief from her handbag.

And then, from her handbag, she produced a large pen.

Five minutes later she'd finished.

Instead of saying:

YOU ARE NOW ENTERING MISERYLAND
    SMILING
    LAUGHING
    CHUCKLING
    GIGGLING
    FORBIDDEN
    By Order of the King.

Do you know what it said now?

YOU ARE NOW ENTERING LAUGHTERLAND
    SMILING
    LAUGHING
    CHUCKLING
    GIGGLING
    PERMITTED
    By Order of the King

"There," said little Miss Sunshine. "Now you can be happy."

"But I don't know HOW to be happy," sniffed the King.

"I've never TRIED it!"

"Nonsense," said little Miss Sunshine.

"It's really very easy," she smiled.

The King tried a smile.

"Not bad," she laughed.

The King tried a laugh.

"Getting better," she chuckled.

The King tried a chuckle.

"You've got it," she giggled.

The King looked at her.

"So I have," he giggled.

"I'm the King of Laughterland!"

As little Miss Sunshine arrived home, there was Mr Happy out for an evening stroll.

"Hello," he grinned. "Where have you been?"

"Miseryland!" she replied.

"Miseryland?" he said.

"I didn't know there was such a place!"

Little Miss Sunshine giggled.

"Actually," she said.

"There isn't!"